J
Ernst, Kathleen,-Meet Caroline :an Am

Meijer Branch
Jackson District Library   9/12/2012

P9-CAS-890

tape added to back page 12/30/22 BK-MEI

WITHDRAWN

1812

MEET
Caroline
An American Girl

BY KATHLEEN ERNST

ILLUSTRATIONS ROBERT PAPP

VIGNETTES LISA PAPP

★ American Girl®

THE AMERICAN GIRLS

1764  KAYA, an adventurous Nez Perce girl whose deep love for horses and respect for nature nourish her spirit

1774  FELICITY, a spunky, spritely colonial girl, full of energy and independence

1812 CAROLINE, a daring, self-reliant girl who learns to steer a steady course amid the challenges of war

1824  JOSEFINA, a Hispanic girl whose heart and hopes are as big as the New Mexico sky

1853  CÉCILE AND MARIE-GRACE, two girls whose friendship helps them—and New Orleans— survive terrible times

1854  KIRSTEN, a pioneer girl of strength and spirit who settles on the frontier

J
Ernst, Kathleen,-Meet Caroline :an American

Meijer Branch
Jackson District Library

1864  ADDY, a courageous girl determined to be free in the midst of the Civil War

1904 SAMANTHA, a bright Victorian beauty, an orphan raised by her wealthy grandmother

1914 REBECCA, a lively girl with dramatic flair growing up in New York City

1934 KIT, a clever, resourceful girl facing the Great Depression with spirit and determination

1944  MOLLY, who schemes and dreams on the home front during World War Two

1974 JULIE, a fun-loving girl from San Francisco who faces big changes—and creates a few of her own

Published by American Girl Publishing
Copyright © 2012 by American Girl

All rights reserved. No part of this book may be used or reproduced in
any manner whatsoever without written permission except in the case of
brief quotations embodied in critical articles and reviews.

Questions or comments? Call 1-800-845-0005, visit **americangirl.com**,
or write to Customer Service, American Girl, 8400 Fairway Place,
Middleton, WI 53562-0497.

Printed in China
12 13 14 15 16 17 LEO 10 9 8 7 6 5 4 3 2 1

All American Girl marks, Caroline™, and Caroline Abbott™
are trademarks of American Girl.

This book is a work of fiction. Any similarity to real persons, living or dead, is coincidental
and not intended by American Girl. References to real events, people, or places are used
fictitiously. Other names, characters, places, and incidents are the products of imagination.

Deep appreciation to Constance Barone, Director, Sackets Harbor Battlefield
State Historic Site; Dianne Graves, historian; James Spurr, historian and First Officer,
Friends Good Will, Michigan Maritime Museum; and Stephen Wallace, former Interpretive
Programs Assistant, Sackets Harbor Battlefield State Historic Site.

PICTURE CREDITS

The following individuals and organizations have generously given permission to reprint
images contained in "Looking Back": p. 77—Jacob Eichholtz, *The Ragan Sisters*, 1818, detail.
Gift of Mrs. Cooper R. Drewry, image courtesy of the Board of Trustees, National Gallery of Art,
Washington, D.C.; pp. 78–79—photo by Bruce Litteljohn (Lake Ontario); courtesy of Toronto
Public Library, detail (ship); Mary King, Wooden Doll Museum of the City of New York, Gift of
Dr. Mary Murray Lowden (doll); privately owned (mirror and piano); pp. 80–81—Karen Carr
(map); Library and Archives Canada, Acc. No. 1989-479-5, detail (Iroquois Indians); North Wind
Picture Archives (British capturing American seamen); Picture History (patriotic painting);
pp. 82–83—Naval History and Heritage Command (Woolsey); New York State Office of Parks,
Recreation and Historic Preservation, Bureau of Historic Sites (harbor scene); Print Collection,
Miriam and Ira D. Wallach Division of Art, Prints and Photographs, The New York Public Library,
Astor, Lenox and Tilden Foundations (ship under construction).

Cataloging-in-Publication Data available from the Library of Congress

FOR ALL THE READERS WHO
LOVE HISTORY AND STORIES
AS MUCH AS I DO

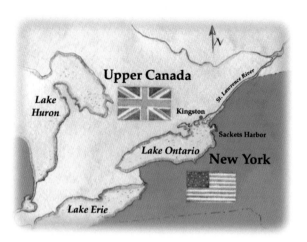

Caroline Abbott is growing up in Sackets Harbor, New York, right on the shore of Lake Ontario. Just across the lake is the British colony of *Upper Canada*.

In 1812, the nation of Canada didn't exist yet. Instead, the lands north of the Great Lakes were still a collection of British colonies. Today, Upper Canada is the Canadian province of Ontario.

In Caroline's time, there was a colony called *Lower Canada*, too. It stretched from Upper Canada eastward to the Atlantic Ocean. Today, it's the province of Quebec.

TABLE OF CONTENTS

CAROLINE'S FAMILY AND FRIENDS

CAROLINE'S FAMILY

PAPA
Caroline's father, a fine shipbuilder who owns Abbott's Shipyard

MAMA
Caroline's mother, a firm but understanding woman

CAROLINE
A daring girl who wants to be captain of her own ship one day

GRANDMOTHER
Mama's widowed mother, who makes her home with the Abbott family

LYDIA
Caroline's eleven-year-old cousin and good friend, who lives in Upper Canada

MRS. SHAW
*A neighbor who
sometimes finds fault
with Caroline*

MR. TATE
*The chief carpenter at
Abbott's, and a good friend
of Caroline's family*

SETH
*A young post walker who
delivers mail to nearby
farms and villages*

HOSEA BARTON
*A skilled sailmaker at
Abbott's Shipyard*

A FINE SLOOP

 Caroline Abbott leaned over the rail
and laughed with delight. "Isn't this
wonderful?" she asked her cousin Lydia.
Sailing on Lake Ontario was fun any time, but being
permitted to come aboard the sloop *White Gull* on its
very first voyage was an extra-special treat.

"It's marvelous," Lydia agreed. "I'm glad that
Oliver and your papa invited us."

Caroline's father had built *White Gull* for Oliver,
Lydia's older brother. "You're lucky to get command
of such a fine little sloop," Caroline told Oliver, who
was steering the ship.

"*White Gull* still belongs to your father," Oliver
reminded her. "It will take me some time to earn

1

enough money to pay him back." His voice dropped. "I just hope America doesn't decide to go to war with Great Britain before I can do so," he muttered.

"Let's not talk about that today!" Lydia said impatiently.

Caroline felt impatient, too. She'd listened to adults arguing about whether America should declare war on Great Britain all her life. Caroline didn't want a war. She didn't even want to *think* about a war.

The breeze whipped some strands of hair into Oliver's face. He paused to retie his hair behind his neck. "It's been thirty years since America won its independence from Britain. Maybe President Madison can avoid fighting another war."

Caroline wanted to change the conversation from war to a happier topic. "Now that the sloop is finished, you can sail all around Lake Ontario!"

Oliver grinned. "I'm looking forward to buying and selling goods along the lakeshore. It's a fine way to earn a living."

"You can start by buying some embroidery silk for me!" Caroline said.

Oliver shook his head. "Mistress Abbott, I will

gladly haul sailcloth and tar for your father, and apples and potatoes for farmers. I will happily carry mail, and take passengers wherever they wish to go. But surely you cannot expect me to shop for embroidery silk!"

Caroline smiled mischievously. "I need something of a reddish brown. Like cinnamon, but with more red."

Lydia giggled as Oliver made a face.

"And *then*, some lace," Caroline continued. "Mama is helping me make a new dress for my tenth birthday. A bit of new lace would be perfect."

"Enough teasing," Oliver begged. "I'm a merchant, not a lady's maid!"

"Why do you think I'm teasing?" Caroline asked. She held her head high, the way Lydia did when she was pretending to be a fancy lady. Lydia, who was almost twelve, giggled even harder.

"Oliver?" Papa called in his no-nonsense captain voice. "Watch that you stay on course. And you girls—remember to stay clear of the mainsail."

"We'll stay clear," Caroline promised. Really, Papa didn't need to remind her about every little thing! She'd been born on the shore of Lake Ontario,

3

and she'd been sailing with him for as long as she could remember. Papa was the finest shipbuilder on all the Great Lakes. And one day . . .

"What are you thinking about?" Lydia asked. "You have a dreamy look on your face."

Caroline hesitated before bursting out with it. "One day, I'm going to ask Papa to build *me* a sloop. I'll be captain." It was her most precious wish, one she usually kept tucked away in her heart.

Beneath her bonnet, Lydia's eyes went wide with surprise. "You can't be captain of a ship!"

"I *shall* be," Caroline insisted. "After I finish learning to be a good sailor. Would you like to be on my crew? We'll sail all the way to China!"

"China?" Lydia squealed. Neither girl had traveled farther than back and forth across Lake Ontario.

"Yes, China," Caroline declared. "We'll visit the markets there and bring back gifts for our families."

Lydia shook her head. "I don't think I want to go to China," she said. "I want to get married and live in a fine house in Kingston and have six children. All girls."

"Well, then, I will have to bring back *lots* of gifts,"
Caroline said. "Dolls and fancy hair combs and
pretty bowls for your daughters' oatmeal."

"And a silk shawl for me?" Lydia asked.

"Yes," Caroline promised. Then she turned to
look at Oliver. He stood at the back of the boat with
feet braced. He leaned into the tiller, a long wooden
bar used to steer the ship. The
breeze ruffled his hair as he
looked over the lake.

Caroline couldn't hold in
a little sigh. There was no finer
feeling than being aboard a sloop on a fair day.
Sailing made Caroline feel as free as one of the gulls
soaring overhead! She had tried not to envy Oliver
while the men at Papa's shipyard built *White Gull*.
It had been difficult, though. Sometimes envy sat
in her chest like a cold, hard lump.

"Wind's shifting," Papa called.

"Yes, sir," Oliver said. He edged the tiller over
a little farther. The sails made satisfying snapping
sounds as the heavy cloth caught the breeze. Since
the ship held no cargo today, it skimmed lightly over
the waves.

"Caroline, what direction is the wind coming from?" Papa asked.

Caroline closed her eyes, trying to tune her senses to the day as Papa had taught her. She could smell the water, and the faint tang of newly dried paint, and the heavier scent of tar. She heard waves slapping the ship's hull, and the familiar rattle of the lines that controlled the sails, and the steady creaking of wooden timbers beneath her feet. And she felt the wind against her face.

She opened her eyes. "The wind's from the west, Papa!" she called.

He nodded. Caroline felt the lump of envy in her chest melt away. *I can make Papa proud of me,* she thought. If she kept learning all she could about sailing, perhaps one day he would build her a sloop of her very own.

"I feel as if we're flying," Lydia exclaimed. She leaned over the rail, watching the water rush by below. "We might as well be on a flying carpet!"

"*White Gull* is certainly colorful enough to be taken for one," Papa grumbled.

Caroline hid her smile. Papa liked to paint his ships a plain gray. After many discussions, though,

Oliver had convinced Papa to paint this ship bright blue, red, and yellow. Oliver wanted his future customers to recognize his ship easily, even from far away.

Lydia straightened and tugged on the brim of her bonnet. "It is very bright today," she complained.

"I like it." Caroline tipped her head back so that she could feel the June sunshine on her face. The winters in northern New York were long and cold. Caroline didn't see what harm it did to enjoy the sunshine while they had it.

"Young ladies must protect their skin from the sun," Lydia said.

Caroline sighed. Lydia sounded as prim as Mrs. Shaw, a neighbor who was fond of finding fault with Caroline. Lately, Lydia had started acting as if she wanted to be all grown up. Caroline wished Lydia would forget about fancy manners—at least for a little while. She reached inside the small knitted bag she'd carried on board. "Look what I brought!" She pulled out a small top, made of wood and painted green.

"Can we play with it on board?" Lydia asked doubtfully. The girls had spent many hours practicing with it on land, perfecting their ability to make the top spin.

"We can try," Caroline said. "Let's go up near the bow. That's the front," she added, remembering that Lydia didn't know ships as well as she did. "And don't forget—always keep one hand on the rail for safety."

After making their way forward, the girls sat down a short distance apart. Caroline paused, feeling the deck tilt back and forth beneath her. She tried to time her spin, aiming the top so that it would travel down the slope to Lydia.

"Got it!" Lydia cried, snatching the top before it wobbled out of reach. "Now let me try."

With some practice, both girls were soon using the ship's movement to help send the top exactly where they wanted it to go. Caroline grinned when Lydia pushed her bonnet back to get a better view of the top spinning across the deck. Maybe Lydia wasn't *quite* ready to be all grown up after all.

Papa interrupted Caroline's thoughts. "Are you paying attention to the wind?" he called to Oliver. "You need to change the mainsail."

"Yes, sir," Oliver answered. "I'll do it."

Caroline paused. She knew that sailors had to be aware every minute of the way the changing wind affected the sails. They used the wind to keep the ship heading where they wanted to go. Papa had decided that *White Gull* needed to change course.

"No more play for now," she told Lydia. "Hang on, and stay down!" The girls squeezed against the rail, well out of the way.

Papa stationed himself by the ropes that helped control the huge sail. Oliver began shouting commands that any sailor would understand: "Prepare to jibe! Trim the sheet!"

"He's trying to sound like your father," Lydia whispered.

And one day, Caroline thought, *I shall be the one giving those commands.*

Oliver pushed the tiller hard and let the mainsail begin its swing far out over the water. The sloop shuddered as the wind hit the loose sail. Caroline instinctively clenched the rail with both hands. The top slipped from her fingers. It skittered across the tilting deck.

"Oh!" Caroline gasped. As she reached to grab the toy, she felt the rail slip from the fingers of her other hand. Suddenly she too was skidding across the slanting deck.

"Caroline!" Papa bellowed. Oliver shouted a warning. Lydia screamed.

Caroline was tumbling too fast to answer. Her hands burned as they scraped along the deck. She bounced against a wooden storage box, and pain stabbed through her shoulder.

I must stop! she thought frantically. If she got in Papa's way as he wrestled with the ropes, it could mean disaster for the ship. If she got tangled in the ropes, she could be seriously injured. And the heavy beam at the bottom of the sail, called the boom, was swinging across the deck with enough force to knock into the water anyone and anything in its way. Time seemed to slow as Caroline crashed and rolled across the deck. Finally she bumped against the far-side rail. She wrapped her arms around it and hung on with all her strength as the sail swung out over the waves.

It felt to Caroline as if the wind would yank the sail from the mast altogether—and maybe even overturn the ship! But Oliver had learned well. He knew just how long to wait, just the right moment to move the tiller again. After a lurch, the sloop settled politely on a better course.

Caroline struggled to her feet, keeping one hand clenched on the rail. She felt banged and scraped and bruised all over.

"Are you all right?" Lydia asked, hurrying to join her. Then Papa appeared, and Lydia stepped back. Papa's face looked like a thundercloud.

"I'm all right," Caroline said in a small voice. "And I'm sorry."

"What were you *thinking*?" Papa demanded. "You could have been knocked overboard—or even killed, if the sail had hit you! Haven't I taught you better?"

"Yes, sir," Caroline said miserably. "But—it was an accident! I dropped my top, and I was afraid it might fall into the lake, so I tried to grab it. And then..."

Papa glared at the toy, which had come to rest innocently nearby. He snatched it up and stuffed it into his pocket. "There is no room for such play on the deck of a ship!"

"Yes, sir," Caroline said again. Her lower lip trembled. "I just thought... that is, you and Oliver had everything set, and—"

11

"You must be alert every moment when you're on board a ship!" Papa interrupted. "It's not enough to set sail once. Winds shift constantly, and you must always be ready to adjust your course. Out here, everything can be lost in an instant."

"I understand," Caroline whispered.

Papa shook his head. "I don't believe you do. You're too flighty, Caroline. If you want to sail on the Great Lakes, you must stay *steady*. Watchful, every moment."

Caroline's skin grew hot. Papa turned and made his way back to Oliver.

Oliver gave him the tiller before joining the girls. "Don't feel sad," he told Caroline. His tone was kind. "No harm was done."

"I've disappointed Papa," Caroline said.

"No, you frightened him," Oliver said. "That's why he got angry."

"All that matters is that you didn't get hurt," Lydia added. "Gracious! Perhaps you should stop dreaming about a ship of your own."

I won't, Caroline thought stubbornly, although her heart felt as heavy as an anchor. She'd have to work extra hard now to prove herself to Papa.

Lydia tugged her bonnet forward again and gazed out over the water. They had almost crossed the lake. The roofs of Kingston, in Upper Canada, had come into clear view. "Why doesn't your father just put in for Kingston now? You and I could visit the shops."

"He says we don't have time," Caroline said. "We'll drop you off at the landing below your farm."

Oliver cocked his head, sniffing the air. "The wind's dying," he said.

With all the commotion, Caroline hadn't noticed the shift in the weather. The sails, with no wind to fill them, made flapping sounds. The deck motion had gentled. She darted a look at her father, half hopeful and half fearful. Sometimes, when the wind was no more than a soft breeze, he let her practice steering.

He caught her glance. After a moment, his stern expression softened. He beckoned with one hand. Caroline's heart rose. She hurried to join him at the tiller.

"Thank you, Papa," she said. She braced her feet, grasped the polished wooden tiller carefully, and leaned against it. Papa stepped close behind her, putting one strong, calloused hand on the tiller for

Caroline braced her feet, grasped the polished wooden tiller carefully, and leaned against it. "Ease her over a bit," Papa instructed. "That's it."

guidance and the other on her shoulder. Caroline inhaled his familiar, pleasant scent of pipe tobacco and sunshine, mixed with faint traces of sawdust and turpentine from the shipyard.

"Ease her over a bit," Papa instructed. "That's it."

Caroline concentrated as hard as she could. She could feel the ship beneath her feet, responding to each adjustment.

All too soon, however, the little sloop was barely moving. "We're becalmed," Papa announced. "No trouble, though. The wind will come up again."

Caroline glanced toward Kingston. They'd drawn near enough that she could easily make out the town's wood and stone buildings. Several ships bobbed in Kingston's harbor. Upper Canada was a British colony, just as New York had been years ago, before the United States won its independence.

Papa stepped back, put both hands on Caroline's shoulders, and turned her to face him. "You made a mistake today, daughter."

15

"I know, and I'm *very* sorry." Her words seemed to tumble over each other in their eagerness. "I'll do better, Papa. I *promise*."

"Very well, then." Papa nodded.

"I can be a good sailor, Papa," Caroline said. She wanted so much to make him understand! "I know I can. Would you... do you think you might build a ship for me one day?"

"Now, Caroline." Papa brushed a stray curl back from her face with a gentle thumb. "I know you love sailing as much as I do, but you're just a child. And a girl as well."

"I mean when I'm older," Caroline explained. "I can be a good captain, even if I am a girl!"

Papa looked over the water. Finally he said, "I can't say yes or no today. I'd be a poor father indeed if I made a promise I wasn't sure I could keep! I didn't go into business with Oliver until he'd proved himself capable of it, and he's ten years older than you. Do you understand?"

Caroline looked at her shoes, trying to hide her disappointment. She didn't *want* to understand. She wanted Papa to have confidence in her, and to trust that one day she'd be ready.

Papa lowered himself to the deck. "Sit," he invited Caroline, patting the sun-warmed wood. Caroline settled down beside him, still struggling to bury her hurt feelings. Papa rummaged in his pocket and pulled two lengths of cord free. He handed one to Caroline. "Have I ever shown you how to make a Flemish knot? Here, watch how I do it."

Caroline leaned close, trying to follow along with her own cord as Papa wove the two ends of his cord together.

"No, over and under this way." Papa showed her again.

"I think I've got it," Caroline said after a moment. She tied another Flemish knot, this time on her own. "There!"

"Keep practicing," Papa told her, tapping the cord. "Sailors practice their knots so often that when they need to make one quickly, their hands remember how."

Caroline began another Flemish knot. By the time she'd made three in a row, Lydia and Oliver had joined them.

"Uncle John," Lydia asked, "will you tell us a story?"

Papa began filling the bowl of his pipe with

tobacco from a little pouch. "Well, the first ship
I built was a sloop not too different from this one.
Try to imagine sailing twenty years ago. There
weren't many towns around Lake Ontario then, so
I worked on a big river east of here. After I met and
married Caroline's mother, we worked together on
the ship. Sometimes we just hauled freight. Other
times we carried passengers. We'd anchor up at
night, and there would be singing and even dancing
under the stars."

"Oh," Caroline breathed. "That must have
been lovely."

Papa smiled. "It was a fine life. Sloop captains
would pull up alongside each other to exchange
news. A few times, well after dark, I saw glowing
torches along the river shore. Indians used the
torches as they speared fish at night. And—"

"Uncle John!" Oliver called sharply.

Papa scrambled to his feet.

"Has the wind picked up?" Caroline asked,
although she could tell it had not—not very much,
anyway. Then she heard a splash. It came from the
Kingston side of the ship. She followed the others
to the rail.

Three longboats were coming straight toward
White Gull. Even from this distance, Caroline could
see the British flag hanging limply over the boat.
The men pulling on the oars wore blue and white
uniforms. Each boat held about twenty men.

"Why are they working so hard to reach us?"
Caroline asked.

Papa crossed his arms over his chest, frowning.
"Something's wrong," he muttered. "I don't like
this at all."

CHAPTER
TWO
—

TERRIBLE NEWS

 Caroline shoved the knotted line into her pocket with suddenly trembling fingers. "Papa?"

"You girls get below and stay there," he ordered.

Caroline and Lydia exchanged a wide-eyed look. Caroline's heart fluttered as she hurried down the steps to *White Gull's* hold beneath the deck. There was a tiny galley for cooking, a couple of bunks, and empty shelves where Oliver would store barrels of flour and potatoes and whatever else he might haul.

Lydia followed her below. "What do you think is wrong?"

"I can't imagine!" Caroline said. For a few moments the girls waited in uneasy silence. Then

20

Caroline turned back toward the steps.

"Caroline, stop!" Lydia hissed. "Your papa said—"

"I'm not going up on the deck," Caroline said in a low voice. She crept up the steps, crouching at the top so that she could listen.

"What's happening?" Lydia asked in a hoarse whisper.

"The British men are pulling closer," Caroline reported. "I can hear the little splashes from their oars."

A shout cut the afternoon: "*White Gull*! Strike your sails and prepare to be boarded!"

Caroline frowned. The British men were acting as if they owned all of Lake Ontario!

Papa's voice was forceful but calm. "What is your business with us?"

"Sir!" It was the same voice. "Prepare to be boarded at once, or we will open fire!"

Lydia gasped, and Caroline's mouth went dry. Open *fire*? Why would the British men threaten to shoot? Papa and Oliver hadn't done anything wrong!

She peeked around the corner just as the *Gull*'s wood-and-rope ladder clattered against the ship's hull. A moment later, a tall hat popped above the rail. Then the man wearing that hat appeared, in a blue and white uniform coat with gold buttons. He swung one leg over the rail and jumped to the deck. Several sailors climbed on board after him.

"Explain yourself!" Papa demanded.

The British officer lifted his chin, looking haughty. "I am Lieutenant Morris. I—"

"We are an unarmed ship from Sackets Harbor," Oliver interrupted. "We're not carrying cargo."

Go away, Caroline ordered the British man silently. *Just go away!*

Papa planted his feet a little more firmly on the deck. "You have no right to threaten this vessel."

The British officer let one hand rest on the hilt of the long sword hanging by his side. "I have *every* right, sir," he snapped. "Perhaps you have not yet received the news."

"What news?" Papa's tone was hard. Caroline could tell that he was very angry.

The British officer gave him a small, cold smile. "Why, of war, sir."

War? Caroline's stomach clenched. She heard Lydia gasp.

Lieutenant Morris paced a few steps, studying the sloop. "Your American president has declared war on Great Britain," he continued. "I am seizing this vessel in the name of His Majesty King George the Third. You are now my prisoners."

No! Caroline wanted to scream. *No, no, no!* But the words felt frozen inside.

"My father is a British citizen who lives in Upper Canada!" Oliver cried. "You have no cause to seize this ship."

"This ship is flying an American flag," said Lieutenant Morris. "My duty is clear."

Oliver launched himself forward with an angry snarl. Caroline's heart seemed to leap into her throat as the British sailors reached for their weapons.

Papa managed to grab Oliver. "Think of the girls," Papa muttered.

Oliver instantly went still.

"We have two young ladies aboard," Papa told Lieutenant Morris. "I trust that my daughter will be safely returned to her mother in Sackets Harbor. At *once*. And—"

"Papa, no!" Caroline cried. All the men's heads turned as she scrambled into the open.

23

"Caroline, be still," Papa said in a voice so stern that she swallowed her protests.

Then Papa turned back to the British officer. "And my young niece lives not three miles from here. Will you make provisions for the girls?"

"Why—why, of course." Lieutenant Morris's voice had lost its mocking tone. "Your niece will be given safe haven in Kingston until her parents can fetch her. I will escort your daughter back to Sackets Harbor myself, under a flag of truce. I give you my word."

Papa left the knot of men and crouched in front of Caroline. "I know what's best, daughter," he said, taking her hands in his.

"I don't want to go with them," Caroline whispered.

"I know," he said gently. "But you must obey me, and be brave."

Caroline stared at Papa through tears. She didn't feel brave at all. Lydia had come on deck behind her, and she stood clinging to her brother. Lydia looked as if she wasn't feeling brave, either.

"Remember, you are a sailor's daughter," Papa told Caroline. "Everyone must sometimes face stormy seas. Good sailors learn to ride the storms through to better weather. Can you do that?"

"I—I'll try."

"Stay steady, Caroline. Obey your mama. Give her and your grandmother whatever help they need while I'm away." Papa's voice was urgent. "I must have your *promise*."

Caroline swiped at her eyes with one hand. "I promise, Papa."

"Make me proud." Papa squeezed her hands before rising. He looked at the lieutenant. "Let's get on with it."

As Lieutenant Morris snapped some orders to his men, Lydia gave Caroline a fierce hug. "Good-bye," she whispered in Caroline's ear.

"Good-bye," Caroline echoed. She felt numb inside. When would she see Lydia again? When would she see *any* of them again?

Lieutenant Morris pointed to the longboat still bobbing right beside *White Gull*. "If you please, child," he said to Caroline.

Caroline wanted to yell, *I am not your child!* But her voice seemed locked inside her throat again. The best she could do was ignore the helping hand he offered. She climbed down the ladder into the longboat. Her knuckles got scraped, and she had to kick her skirt aside as she planted her feet on the rungs. Once she was in the vessel, she sat with her knees pulled up close and shoulders hunched, staring at her lap.

Lieutenant Morris and some of his sailors came down the ladder and settled into the longboat. Caroline felt the boat lurch forward when the sailors began pulling on the heavy oars. As the longboat moved away from *White Gull,* she couldn't help looking over her shoulder. Papa sat straight as a mast in one of the other longboats. Lydia was climbing down the ladder to join him, and Oliver waited his turn. The British sailors dropped the *Gull's* sails.

Caroline felt an ache inside her chest. One tear spilled over and slid down her cheek. She swiped it fiercely and bent her head again. *I will not cry,* she told herself, over and over. *I will not let them see me cry.*

CHAPTER
THREE
—

A SAD HOMECOMING

Soon the wind picked up, and the British men were able to raise a small sail in the longboat. Caroline kept her head lowered, refusing to look at the sailors who had taken her father prisoner and stolen *White Gull*. After what seemed like forever, she heard the rattle of rigging lines banging lightly against the masts of several anchored ships, and she knew they must be approaching Sackets Harbor. She was home.

She looked up. The little village of Sackets Harbor sat on the shore of a natural harbor, protected from Lake Ontario's sometimes-fierce wind and waves by a protective curl of land.

A little log blockhouse perched on a rise.
That was where American soldiers watched
over the port and protected its ships.
Caroline hoped that the Americans
would come and arrest Lieutenant Morris!

As she watched, the Abbotts' house came into
view up the hill from the harbor, on the eastern
edge of the village. Caroline pictured
Mama and Grandmother inside,
polishing pewter or cleaning
fish for supper, not knowing
what terrible thing had happened.

"Show us where to land, child," Lieutenant
Morris called. He pulled a large white handkerchief
from his pocket and waved it above his head.
Caroline knew that white handkerchiefs or flags were
used to signal a truce. The lieutenant was telling the
American soldiers not to shoot.

Caroline pointed toward the dock at Papa's
shipyard. Just knowing that Papa's workers were
nearby made her feel safer.

The longboat moved through the harbor. On
the American navy ship *Oneida*, which was anchored
there, sailors gathered at the rail to watch. Two

Seneca Indian men canoeing past with baskets of whitefish to sell stopped paddling and stared. Caroline heard shouts from the landing. Several workmen lifted their heads and pointed.

Lieutenant Morris's sailors maneuvered the longboat beside a wooden ladder nailed to Papa's dock. Caroline jerked up her skirt with one hand and half-stepped, half-tumbled over the side of the longboat. Her foot slipped from the rung she'd aimed for. Icy water clamped around her leg, knee-deep.

One of the British men held out his hand to her. "Here, now, let me help you," he said.

"I don't want your help!" Caroline yelled. She clenched the ladder and managed to find a foothold. Climbing up a ladder in a wet skirt was even harder than climbing down.

The dock trembled beneath heavy footsteps as Papa's chief carpenter ran to meet her. "What's this?" Mr. Tate demanded. "Miss Caroline?"

"I have delivered the young lady," Lieutenant Morris shouted, waving his handkerchief again as the longboat pulled away. "As I promised her father I would."

Caroline glared at the lieutenant. "We didn't even

One of the British men held out his hand to her.
"I don't want your help!" Caroline yelled.

know that a war had started!" she shouted after him. "What you did is not *fair!*"

"War?" Mr. Tate stared at the departing longboat. "*War*, you say?"

"President Madison has declared war on Britain!" she told him. "That British officer took Papa and Oliver prisoner, and seized *White Gull!*"

Mr. Tate sputtered, "Why, those—I could just..." His hands clenched into fists.

Caroline grabbed his arm. "I have to find Mama, but please—go tell the navy men. Before some other American ship gets captured."

He gave one grim nod and pounded down the dock. Caroline ran after him, shoes squishing, her clammy skirt clinging to her legs. She ran through the shipyard and past the warehouses, shops, and market stalls near the harbor. Turning up the hill, she dodged a man balancing a large toolbox on one shoulder and a woman selling candles from a tray. "Isn't that the Abbott girl?" someone asked. Caroline kept running.

Her lungs felt ready to burst by the time she'd run up Main Street's hill and turned left onto the lane that led to her own home. She passed the Shaw house, and finally—up ahead was her home. And there was Mama, cutting rhubarb in the garden.

"Mama!" Caroline croaked.

Mama glanced up, then scrambled to her feet and ran to meet her daughter. "Caroline? What is it?" She grabbed Caroline's shoulders. "What's wrong?"

Caroline's words came out in breathless bursts. "The British... took Papa... prisoner! Oliver, too."

Mama turned pale. *"What?"*

"And they stole *White Gull*. They said we're at war!"

Mama clutched Caroline close in a tight embrace. "Heaven protect us."

Half an hour later, Grandmother put a cup of steaming ginger tea on the table in front of Caroline. "Drink up," she ordered. She was a white-haired woman with stooped shoulders who moved a little more slowly with every passing year. Her blue eyes could spark with impatience, though. Caroline picked up the cup and sipped.

Mama was striding back and forth, her heels

clicking angrily against the floorboards. "How dare
they!" she muttered again.

Grandmother sat down in her chair by the
kitchen fireplace, where she could warm her bones.
"There is nothing the British won't dare," she said
quietly. Caroline knew that Grandmother was
thinking about her husband, who had died fighting
for America's independence during the Revolutionary War.

Mama stopped pacing and looked from
Grandmother to Caroline. Her voice was as firm
as an oak plank. "Thirty years ago, British soldiers
killed my father," she said. "I will *not* allow British
soldiers to imprison my husband and nephew now.
Not without trying to win their freedom. Do you
hear me?"

"Yes, ma'am," Caroline whispered. Still, she
didn't see that she and Mama and Grandmother had
any choice. Papa, Oliver, and *White Gull* were gone.
And Caroline was desperately afraid that she would
never see any of them again.

Caroline jumped when someone knocked on the back door a moment later. The young man who stepped inside was all long arms and long legs, and skinny as a fence rail.

"Seth, I'm so glad to see you," Caroline said. Seth Whittleslee was only a few years older than Caroline. He was the local post walker, tramping up and down the lakeshore delivering news and mail. Sometimes he even crossed the border into Upper Canada, so Caroline was never sure when she'd see her friend next. When he could spare a day, though, he and Caroline went fishing together.

"Is it true?" Seth demanded. "I just heard that the British seized *White Gull* and took your father and Oliver and Lydia prisoner!"

"They said Lydia could go home. But the rest is true." Caroline quickly told her friend what had happened.

"Well, I think it's high time for war," Seth muttered. "The British have never respected our American border. They interfere with our trade.

And everyone says they encourage some of the Indian tribes to cause trouble."

"For years they've been kidnapping American sailors on the Atlantic Ocean and forcing them to join the British navy," Grandmother added.

"And now they've kidnapped Papa and Oliver," Caroline said. She slid one hand into her pocket and clenched the cord, now thick with Flemish knots, that Papa had given her.

Mama began to pace again. "I wish I had a way to send a message to Aaron and Martha in Upper Canada, but now . . ." Her voice trailed away.

Caroline understood Mama's worry. Uncle Aaron and Aunt Martha, Oliver and Lydia's parents, had moved their family from New York to Upper Canada several years earlier.

"I can take a message to them," Seth offered.

Caroline's eyes widened. "Is it still safe for you to go to Upper Canada now that we're at war?"

"I have several letters that need to be delivered there," Seth said with determination. "People are depending on me. I'll make sure Lydia's safe at home with her parents."

"But you're an American," Caroline said. She

turned to her mother. "If Seth goes to Canada, won't the British arrest him, too?"

"I don't think so," Mama replied. "*White Gull* attracted attention because it was flying an American flag."

"And because both sides are desperate for ships," Seth added. "People are saying that whichever side can control the Great Lakes will likely win the war."

"Still, we don't know what's happening over there." Mama looked Seth in the eye. "We're grateful for your kindness, but you must be careful."

"I will," Seth promised. "I'll head northeast to the Saint Lawrence River. I know someone with a small fishing boat who can get me across. We won't fly any flag at all."

"Good luck," Caroline said. "And thank you."

Seth started toward the door, but then he turned back to Mrs. Abbott. "I almost forgot! I was at Porter's warehouse earlier. He said to tell you that the carpet you ordered arrived this morning. He'll have his men bring it around."

After Seth had left, Grandmother spoke. "It may be best to have Porter send the carpet back. That may be a luxury you can no longer afford." She looked at her granddaughter. "I'm sorry, Caroline. I know it was meant for your bedroom."

It took Caroline a moment to understand why Grandmother was concerned. Then she remembered that Papa had purchased the lumber and supplies needed to build *White Gull,* and the ship had been seized before Oliver could make even one trading trip and begin to pay Papa back. And now Papa and Oliver were prisoners, and no one knew how long they'd be held. How would Mama pay the bills? Would Abbott's Shipyard close? Would Mama have to sell their house? How would they even buy food?

"No." Mama put her hands on her hips. "We will keep the carpet. The British have done enough damage without denying my daughter a carpet to warm her feet this winter!" She looked so fierce that, in spite of everything, Caroline felt her lips curl in a tiny smile.

"Now, then," Mama continued. "Let's think about what must be done."

Grandmother leaned over and added another small log to the fire. "You need to see to the shipyard."

"And you could talk to the navy men in Sackets Harbor," Caroline suggested hopefully. "Lieutenant Woolsey, isn't that the man in charge? Maybe he'll launch a raid on Kingston and get Papa and Oliver back home."

Mama nodded. "You're both right. I'll go down to the shipyard first. I don't want the men wondering if they're about to lose their jobs." She whipped off her gardening apron and quickly scrubbed most of the mud from beneath her fingernails. "Caroline, stay here and help your grandmother. The carpet will be delivered this afternoon, and there's supper to fix."

"But I don't want—" Caroline began. Then she stopped. She didn't want to stay home and worry while Mama went to the shipyard. But she could still hear an echo of Papa's voice: *Stay steady, Caroline. Obey your mama. Give her and your grandmother whatever help they need while I'm away.*

Caroline thought about that, trying to decide what was best. Finally she said, "I can stay and help Grandmother, but I might also be able to help you at the shipyard. I know where Papa keeps his books, and I know all the men by name."

Caroline said, "I can stay and help Grandmother, but I might also be able to help you at the shipyard. I know where Papa keeps his books."

39

Grandmother nodded approvingly. "I'm fine here alone."

Mama paused, and then reached for her shawl. "Very well. Caroline, come with me."

CHAPTER
FOUR
—

LIEUTENANT
WOOLSEY

Caroline had to hurry to keep up
with Mama as they headed out.
Caroline was glad that her bossy
neighbor wasn't in sight. Mrs. Shaw had once told
Caroline's mother that Papa spent too much time
with Caroline. "It's clear that Mr. Abbott adores his
daughter," Mrs. Shaw had said, "but do you think
it's wise to let Caroline spend so much time at the
shipyard? A daughter's place is in the home,
learning cooking and needlework."

   "There are many girls twice her age who aren't
as skilled at needlework," Mama had said crisply.
At the time, Caroline had ignored Mrs. Shaw's
comments. Today, she wasn't sure she'd be able to.

The village seemed to crackle with worried excitement. Passersby jostled Caroline as she and Mama made their way past homes and shops. A few warehouses stood nearer the water, filled with crates and barrels of goods—window glass, boots, china teapots, books, chocolate. The roads leading from Sackets Harbor to inland New York were narrow, rutted, and barely passable for much of the year. Almost all supplies came and went by ship.

Caroline felt a painful little lurch in her chest as they came to the wooden sign, painted with a graceful sloop, that simply said "Abbott's." An almost-finished schooner towered over their heads on a slipway—a narrow log bed near the water's edge from which the finished ship would be launched. The skeleton of another ship was rising up on heavy wooden support posts. Ladders leaned against the hull, and scraps of wood littered the ground. No carpenters were in sight, though. No one bustled past pushing a wheelbarrow or hauling lumber. No one shouted orders, or pounded with his hammer, or sang old songs.

42

They found Mr. Tate and a dozen other workers in the carpentry shop. Each man had a special skill. Some men worked with wood, some filled the seams between planks to make ships watertight, some prepared the ropes that sailors used to handle the sails. The men fell silent as Mama and Caroline stepped into the shop.

"Good afternoon, gentlemen," Mama said. "I can see that you've already heard the sorry news."

Mr. Tate tugged the lock of hair that fell over his forehead, a sailor's traditional gesture of respect. "Forgive me if I spoke out of turn, Mrs. Abbott, but I felt the men should know."

"Of course." Mama took a deep breath and squared her shoulders. "I don't know how long my husband will be away. And I don't know what the war will mean for our business."

The men exchanged troubled glances. Then Hosea Barton, the sailmaker, stepped forward. His skin was as brown as mahogany, and Caroline had always loved to watch his strong, dark fingers working against the pale sailcloth. "Pardon me, ma'am," he said. "Are we out of work?"

"No, you are not," Mama said firmly. "Abbott's

43

has promised to complete those two schooners outside, and we will not disappoint our customers. Mr. Tate, do you have everything you need to continue?"

"Why . . . yes, ma'am!"

"Good. You are in charge until Mr. Abbott returns."

Jed, the youngest woodworker, spoke up. "What happens if Mr. Abbott doesn't come back?"

"Papa *will* be back!" Caroline glared at Jed. The workshop went completely quiet. Jed flushed and looked at his shoes. For a moment the only sound was the noisy cries of gulls outside, fighting over fish scraps.

Then Mama looked Jed in the eye. "Of course Mr. Abbott will return," she said, quietly but firmly. "Now, you may all get back to work."

The men began heading to the door. Samuel, the ropemaker's apprentice, paused to say, "Thank you, ma'am. We'll do Mr. Abbott proud."

When the other men were gone, Mr. Tate shifted his weight uneasily from one foot to the other. "Mrs. Abbott," he began in a low voice, "I can manage the men. But there's the account books . . ."

44

"I kept the books when Mr. Abbott and I began the business," Mama said. "I can do so again."

Mr. Tate looked surprised and then relieved. "Yes, ma'am," he said.

Mama took Caroline's hand. "Come along. I need to look at Papa's business papers."

When Caroline reached the doorway of Papa's empty office, her feet stopped moving. The air still smelled of his spicy blend of pipe tobacco. The design drawings he'd made for the two schooners were tacked up on one wall. His favorite tankard sat on the desk. Caroline longed to blink and see Papa hard at work among his things. But he was not there.

Finally she followed Mama into the room. Mama touched a model of the first sloop Papa had ever built. Suddenly Caroline felt Mama shudder as she gulped down a sob.

For a moment Caroline wanted to cry, too. Instead she slipped her hand into her mother's. "You can keep the business going, Mama. I know you can. And ... I can help you." She wasn't sure how, but she was determined to try.

Mama wiped her eyes and gave Caroline a watery smile. "You know where Papa keeps the ledger?"

45

"Yes. Right here." Caroline opened a wooden box on the desk and pulled out a leather-bound book. "Contracts for those two schooners are here, and he keeps bills in this drawer."

"Goodness," Mama said. "How fortunate that you've spent so much time helping your father."

"But I don't know anything important," Caroline said sadly. "Sometimes I copied a bill or letter for Papa. Or I tidied up his office, or I read to the men as they worked. That's all." None of that would be of help now.

"I'll sort it out," Mama assured her. She squinted at the lines of Papa's slanting script. "I hope that—"

The door burst open. Caroline gave a little squeak of surprise as Lieutenant Woolsey himself stepped inside. He didn't look much older than Oliver, but he'd been stationed in Sackets Harbor for several years, enforcing trade laws and capturing smugglers. He had curly hair swept back from his face, and side-whiskers that stretched along his jaw. His blue uniform coat glittered with gold lace and buttons and braid.

Lieutenant Woolsey quickly pulled off his hat. "Are you Mrs. Abbott?"

"I am," Mama said. "And this is my daughter, Caroline. Thank you for coming so quickly."

Lieutenant Woolsey looked confused. "For coming quickly?"

"Aren't you here because of my husband?"

"Well, yes, ma'am. I have some business to discuss with him." He tapped his leg impatiently. "With the news that war has been declared, that business is quite urgent. Is he here?"

"The British took him prisoner!" Caroline burst out. "And they stole our new sloop."

The lieutenant's eyebrows rose in surprise. "Mr. Abbott was sailing *White Gull*? I'd heard another name—Oliver Livingston."

"Oliver is my brother's son," Mama told him. "He was to captain the sloop. My daughter was there as well. Caroline, perhaps you should tell Lieutenant Woolsey what happened."

Caroline explained as quickly and clearly as she could. "So you see, sir," she concluded, "we need you to get Papa and Oliver back. And the sloop, too."

Lieutenant Woolsey rubbed his chin with one knuckle. He did not reply.

Caroline felt her heart grow heavier. "Won't you

help us?" she asked. "Can't you send navy men to Kingston?"

He began turning his hat in his hands. "It's not that simple. I have no idea where the British have taken your father and cousin, and—"

"My Uncle Aaron could probably find out," Caroline said. She saw Mama's small frown and knew it was because she'd interrupted, but the words kept pouring out. "He and Aunt Martha and my cousin Lydia live in Upper Canada. If he can find out where the British are holding Papa and Oliver, will you go get them back? *Please?*"

Lieutenant Woolsey sighed. "I wish there were something I could do, but—"

"My husband was captured before news of the war had even reached us," Mama said sharply, "and you propose to do nothing?"

"On the contrary, ma'am, I am doing all I can," he retorted. "Now that war has been declared, keeping Lake Ontario safe for ships is of great importance to the United States. My first priority is to strengthen our defenses here against possible attack. I've already alerted our soldiers to be on guard."

Caroline's eyes widened. The British might attack Sackets Harbor?

"We need to build a fleet with all speed," the lieutenant was saying. "I've heard that Mr. Abbott is quite skilled."

"He is," Caroline said fiercely.

"We're starting a navy shipyard here. However, the workers haven't arrived yet." Lieutenant Woolsey shoved a hand through his hair. "Mrs. Abbott, I was going to ask your husband to build a gunboat for the navy. But now that he's been captured—"

"Nothing has changed," Mama said firmly. "Abbott's Shipyard still employs the finest craftsmen you could hope to find. I am managing the yard while my husband is away. And yes, we will build a gunboat for you."

Lieutenant Woolsey twisted his hat more forcefully. *He'll ruin that hat if he's not careful,* Caroline thought.

"Will your workers know what to do without Mr. Abbott?" he asked finally. "The British in Kingston are already at work on their own ships. We *must* not let them get ahead of us. Your men aren't used to building ships that can carry heavy cannons. Even

49

the sails will be different, made of heavier cloth."

Caroline felt her impatience growing. "The men can build big ships! And Hosea Barton—he's our sailmaker—he's the best on the lakes!"

Mama put a hand on Caroline's shoulder and squeezed, as if to say, *That's enough, now.* Caroline pinched her lips together.

"I see," Lieutenant Woolsey said. The hat turned another circle in his hands.

"My daughter is correct, sir," Mama said. "Our workers can do whatever needs doing."

"Very well, then," the lieutenant said. "Do you have a lawyer? Someone whom your husband would trust to sign a contract?"

Mama's eyebrows rose. "My husband would trust *me,* sir. I will sign whatever documents are required. After I have reviewed them, of course, and we have agreed to whatever changes might be necessary. Draw them up and have them delivered here."

He nodded, made an attempt to smooth his hat, and planted it back on his head. "Thank you, Mrs. Abbott." He looked from Caroline to Mama. "I *am* sorry about what happened today, but I suspect you'll get good news soon. Your men were not members of the military, nor smugglers. I'm sure that the British will release them."

"When?" Caroline demanded. "Today?"

"Well, perhaps not today," he said. "I'm afraid you must simply be patient and wait." With that, Lieutenant Woolsey walked out the door.

Grandmother's Advice

As Caroline and her mother walked past the Shaw house on their way home, the front door flew open. Mrs. Shaw hurried down the gravel path and crushed Caroline into a hug. "Oh, you poor, poor child."

Her pity didn't make Caroline feel any better. Mrs. Shaw was a plump woman, with a round face that Caroline thought only *looked* kind. She wriggled free from her neighbor's arms.

"Lieutenant Woolsey believes the British will release my husband soon," Mama said.

"He knows best," Mrs. Shaw replied.

"Perhaps." Mama frowned. "Actually, though, I think Lieutenant Woolsey is too busy right now

52

to worry about Mr. Abbott and Oliver."

"Well, he has many things to worry about." Mrs. Shaw spread her hands. "We all have much to do to prepare for war. My husband volunteers with the gun crew, you know. Thank heavens they've been practicing."

"Lieutenant Woolsey said Sackets Harbor is poorly defended," Caroline said. Remembering the grim look on the officer's face made her shiver.

"If so, it's not the gun crew's fault," Mrs. Shaw huffed. "The government sent cannonballs that don't even fit their cannons."

"The cannonballs don't fit?" Caroline echoed. "How can we defend ourselves?"

"We must pray that our soldiers will find a solution." Mama pressed her lips together. "Now, Mrs. Shaw, if you will excuse us, Caroline and I should get home."

Mrs. Shaw put a hand on Mama's arm. "What will happen to the shipyard?"

"Mama is taking charge until Papa gets back," Caroline told her.

Mrs. Shaw looked at Mama. "I can't imagine how you'll manage the shipyard *and* your household!"

"I'm going to help," Caroline said. Couldn't Mrs. Shaw tell that she was only making Mama feel worse?

Mrs. Shaw patted Caroline's shoulder. "I'm sure you mean well, Caroline. But we all know that your kitchen skills are a bit, well . . . lacking."

Caroline flushed. Two days earlier, Mrs. Shaw had stopped by just as Caroline was taking bread out of the bake oven. Grandmother was teaching Caroline how to bake, but somehow, Caroline never seemed able to mix in just the right amount of flour and water, or knead the dough to the perfect silky-smooth texture. Her loaf had turned out heavy and hard.

Now Mama said sharply, "Mrs. Shaw!"

"I don't mean to criticize," Mrs. Shaw said, although Caroline was sure that was *exactly* what she meant to do. "We must all pull together in times like these," the older woman added. "I'd be glad to help teach Caroline."

Oh no, Caroline thought. Her spirits sank lower.

"Thank you for the offer," Mama said. "But we'll do fine. Good afternoon." Caroline and Mama walked the rest of the way in silence.

Once they were home, Caroline let Mama tell Grandmother about the conversation with Lieutenant Woolsey. Caroline plodded up the stairs.

When Caroline reached her small bedroom, she caught her breath. Her carpet had been delivered! Last March, Mama had taken Caroline to look at samples. "Pick out exactly what you want," Mama had said. It was the first time her parents had ever permitted Caroline to make such an important, grown-up decision. She had looked at each sample carefully, feeling the materials and trying to imagine how such a carpet would look in her bedroom. It had been so hard to choose!

Now Caroline knew her choice was perfect. The new carpet was made of thick wool in warm shades of gold and brown. The beautiful carpet, soft and cozy, would make her unheated room feel warmer during Sackets Harbor's icy winters. Even now, on a day when everything had gone so terribly wrong, the carpet was comforting.

Inkpot, her black cat, must have

found the carpet comforting, too. He was curled into a ball in a patch of sunlight, fast asleep. Caroline scooped him up and nestled one cheek against his soft fur. Papa had brought Inkpot home when he was no more than a scruffy stray kitten. "Sailors believe black cats are good luck," he'd told Caroline.

"I wish you'd been on board *White Gull* today," Caroline whispered. "Maybe you would have brought us better luck." Inkpot purred sleepily, and Caroline gently put him down again.

She walked to the little mahogany worktable in the corner. The table had a hinged board where she could write letters, and compartments for bottles of ink and notepaper and blotting sand. A lower drawer had plenty of space for her sewing supplies. A fabric bag slung beneath the worktable held her current project, an embroidered map of Lake Ontario's eastern shoreline from Sackets Harbor around to Kingston.

In an instant, all the pleasure Caroline had taken in her new carpet faded. She'd planned to put the map, when it was finished, into a wooden frame so that Papa could use it as a fire screen. She had loved imagining Papa sitting in his favorite chair by the hearth on frosty winter nights, with the fire screen allowing him to stay warm without getting scorched. When the lake was iced over and Papa couldn't sail, the embroidered map would remind him that spring would come again.

Now Papa was gone, and his fate was unknown. *Will Papa ever even see the map?* Caroline wondered miserably.

She turned and clattered back down the stairs, across the hall, and out the front door. She didn't stop running until Lake Ontario spread below her. To the west, the lake stretched toward a horizon stained pink and orange by the setting sun. Caroline stared in the direction of Kingston. Papa and Oliver were out there, *somewhere*. Had the British put them in jail? Did they have enough to eat? When would they be coming home? The ache in her heart threatened to take her breath away.

The lake was darkening to black when, sometime

later, Caroline heard footsteps. "I roasted some whitefish," Grandmother said as she joined Caroline. "And baked gingerbread."

"I'm not hungry," Caroline told her.

Grandmother planted her cane in front of her and rested both hands on it. "I don't imagine you are," she said. "But you can't fight the British if you don't eat."

"I can't fight the British!" Caroline protested. She hated feeling so angry—and so helpless.

"No, but you can help me tend the house."

Caroline blinked away tears. "I can't even bake bread that's fit to eat."

To her surprise, Grandmother chuckled. "All you need is practice."

Caroline didn't want to practice baking bread, and she didn't want to be at war. "I want things to be as they were this morning," she said.

Grandmother shook her head. "I'm afraid such thoughts are a waste of time, my girl."

I can't help it, Caroline thought. One more protest slipped out: "What happened today just isn't *fair.*"

"Life often isn't fair," Grandmother said. "We can turn bitter and complain about our problems.

Or we can try to change what we may, and make the best of every day we're given."

For a long moment Caroline and Grandmother stood in silence, watching spots of light blink from the village as swallows swooped overhead. Then Caroline said, "I disappointed Papa today. He told me I was too flighty."

"I see," Grandmother said. She sounded thoughtful.

"I wanted to show him that I can do better," Caroline said miserably. "But now the British have taken him! What if I never get the chance?"

"I believe you will," Grandmother said. "But Caroline, think for a moment. I suspect your papa was asking you to be more responsible. That's good advice, whether he's home or not. With your mother working at the shipyard, I'll need more help from you here at home."

Scrubbing floors and weeding gardens won't help bring Papa and Oliver home, Caroline thought. She wanted to do something that would help get them back! But she knew that Grandmother, with all her aches and pains, couldn't manage the house alone.

Caroline looked at the woman standing beside

her. "Grandmother? How did you manage during the Revolution?" With a shiver, she remembered what Lieutenant Woolsey had said about a possible British attack on Sackets Harbor. "Were you ever in the middle of the fighting?"

"Once," Grandmother said.

"Weren't you scared?"

Grandmother stared into the growing shadows. "I was taking water to my husband and his men. I knew how desperately they needed it, and so... I went. I wasn't afraid until later."

"It must have been horrible when Grandfather got killed," Caroline whispered. Those events had always seemed like something from the very distant past to her. Suddenly, they seemed much more real.

"It *was* horrible," Grandmother agreed. "But I had a farm to tend and children to raise. I learned that women can do what they must."

"I'll do my best to help you and Mama," Caroline promised. "But I wish I could do something to help Papa, too. To help fight the British."

"More than anything else, I think, your papa would want you to stay safe," Grandmother said.

"Far away from the British."

Caroline would be grateful if she never saw a British uniform again! But staying away from the British wouldn't help Papa, either. She sighed. "I don't want your bones to get chilled," she told her grandmother. "Let's go back inside."

ATTACK!

Six days later, Seth returned. He had traveled to Upper Canada and back. "Lydia is safe at home," he reported. "Her father is trying to find out where Mr. Abbott and Oliver are being held."

"I'll give Mrs. Abbott the news as soon as she returns from the shipyard," Grandmother said. She and Caroline were sitting in the kitchen, watching Seth gobble warm biscuits and honey. "What's the situation over there?"

"Everything is upside down." Seth caught a drop of honey and licked it from his finger. "People in Upper Canada are terrified that Americans are going to invade. No one knows whether they should hunker down or run for their lives."

"The same thing is happening here," Caroline told him. "Some people have left already." She worked another stitch on her embroidery, pulling the silk thread carefully so that it didn't tangle. Caroline had found that whenever worry threatened to overwhelm her, it helped to keep her hands busy.

Seth finished a third biscuit and got to his feet. "Please excuse me, but I've got a long way to walk yet today."

"Thank you for bringing us news," Caroline told him.

"I was glad to," Seth said. "And Caroline? Try not to worry too much. Your father will likely come home soon."

Caroline wanted to believe her friend. But days inched by, and then weeks. June turned into July. And Papa did not come home.

Every day Caroline's neighbors grew more fearful of a British invasion. And every day Caroline's worry for her father and Oliver was pulled tighter, like a knotted piece of embroidery silk. Uncle Aaron managed to send a letter across the lake in a fishing boat. He wrote that Oliver and Papa were being held in the fort that the British were constructing at Kingston. No one knew how long the two would be kept as prisoners.

Sometimes Caroline went to the shipyard with Mama, where the men were already at work on Lieutenant Woolsey's new gunboat. Sometimes Caroline stayed home with Grandmother, where the garden grew as many weeds as beans and carrots. Always, though, she was waiting for her father— for a glimpse of him hurrying up the hill, for his shout of greeting, for his Papa-scent of tobacco and sawdust, for the feel of his strong hands squeezing hers as if to say, *Well done, Caroline. I'm proud of you.*

One Sunday morning in late July, Caroline took a basket to the garden. A traveling minister was visiting the village, and Grandmother had asked her to pick the ripe peas before they left for the service. Mama had already headed to the shipyard, where the crew was working seven days a week.

As Caroline snapped the first pod from the vine, a *boom* shuddered through the hot morning.

"I suppose the gun crew wants to get their practice in before church, too," she told Inkpot, who was chasing crickets nearby.

Then she heard someone yelling, "Miss Caroline! Miss Caroline!" Samuel, the apprentice ropemaker, burst through the garden gate. His shirt was damp with sweat.

Caroline scrambled to her feet. "What's wrong?" she cried.

"They're coming!" Samuel gasped. He bent over, hands on knees, trying to catch his breath.

Caroline's heart took a hopeful leap. "Papa and Oliver?"

"The *British*!" Another thundering *boom* almost drowned out Samuel's words. "That's the alarm guns, calling in the militia."

Caroline lifted her skirt and ran across the lane toward the lake. "Oh," she gasped. Five ships flying the flag of Great Britain had formed a ragged line and trapped the American ship *Oneida* inside the harbor.

Caroline's hands curled into fists. "If the British take *Oneida*, we won't have any big ships left to protect us!"

Samuel had followed her. "Lieutenant Woolsey tried to sail *Oneida* out of the harbor," he said, "but the British ships cut him off."

Grandmother hobbled up to join them. "Have mercy," she muttered.

"Mrs. Abbott said you're both to hide in the root cellar," Samuel told them.

"What about Mama?" Caroline cried, but Samuel was already loping away.

"Your mama's place is at the shipyard," said Grandmother. "If the British do make land, they'll look for shipbuilding tools and supplies. What they can't carry off, they'll want to burn."

When Caroline imagined British sailors plundering Abbott's Shipyard, she tasted something sour in her throat. A cannon on one of the British ships fired. The noise shivered through the morning. A plume of gray smoke rose from the gun.

Caroline grabbed Grandmother's hand. "We've got to get to the root cellar before a cannonball lands on us! Come along. I'll help you."

Before they'd taken two steps, though, Mrs. Shaw's shrill voice sliced through the air. "Caroline! Mrs. Livingston! I . . . need your . . . help!" she gasped, stumbling across the yard to meet them. Her straw bonnet was dangling by its strings. Dust and sweat streaked her best Sunday dress.

"What's wrong?" Caroline cried.

"My husband's gun crew—the cannonballs they have are too small!" Mrs. Shaw's shoulders were still heaving with the effort of running. "Our men need heavy cloth to wrap around them so they'll fit the cannons."

"Caroline, fetch my winter cloak," Grandmother said.

"Grandmother, no," Caroline protested. It was the warmest thing she owned.

"Fetch it now!" Grandmother ordered. "And your own, and your mother's. *Quickly.*"

Caroline blinked back tears as she ran to the house. Fear made her legs feel wobbly and her mouth feel as dry as cotton. But she was also angry. Grandmother would suffer terribly next winter without her thick wool cloak.

By the time Caroline pounded up the stairs, her

anger felt as hot as coals. She skidded to a stop at her bedroom door, staring at her new carpet as an idea burst into her mind. *Maybe my carpet could be used to wrap the cannonballs!* she thought. Maybe Grandmother wouldn't have to lose her cloak after all.

Caroline turned and ran downstairs. "Mrs. Shaw!" she hollered. "Come help me! Grandmother, can you fetch the wheelbarrow from the garden?"

It took all the strength Caroline and Mrs. Shaw had between them to roll up Caroline's new carpet. They slid the bulky roll down the stairs and wrestled it into the wheelbarrow. The two ends flopped over the sides and dragged in the dirt.

It hurt Caroline's heart to see her beautiful carpet used so roughly. *This is the right thing to do*, she told herself sternly. She squared her shoulders and grasped the wheelbarrow's handles. A gun boomed and Caroline glanced at Grandmother. *If we go*, she thought, *Grandmother will be left to face the attacks alone.* Caroline hesitated, torn between wanting to protect her grandmother and wanting to help the gun crew.

Grandmother seemed to understand. "Go!" she said. "I'll be fine."

Mrs. Shaw was struggling with the carpet.

68

"Caroline, let's fold the roll over like this. If I hold it in place, can you push?"

Another shot exploded from one of the enemy ships as Caroline lifted the wheelbarrow handles and staggered off. She pushed until her hands and arms ached, and then she and Mrs. Shaw traded places. *Hurry, hurry, hurry,* Caroline urged silently, but there was no need to encourage Mrs. Shaw. Caroline could never have imagined her fussy neighbor so grim-faced and determined. *But then I never could have imagined heading for the gun crew while the British fired at Sackets Harbor, either,* she thought.

It was hard going. Groups of militiamen elbowed past—farmers and workmen who had promised to grab their muskets and report for duty when trouble threatened. Someone on a horse galloped by. A woman led a string of children, all lugging bundles and baskets, toward the woods.

Caroline and Mrs. Shaw stumbled past the harbor and on toward the cannons. Sweat rolled into Caroline's eyes. Her back ached. The trip seemed to take forever.

Then Caroline heard men shouting, just ahead. She looked up and saw Lieutenant Woolsey yelling orders to a dozen men scrambling around several cannons. Scraps of cloth—probably someone else's winter cloak—lay on the ground nearby.

"We need help!" Mrs. Shaw shrieked. She dropped the wheelbarrow handles with a little moan and rubbed her hands. Several men ran to help.

Caroline straightened her back and lifted one edge of the carpet. "Will it suit?" she cried.

"I surely hope so," Mr. Shaw said grimly. "Everything we've tried has either been too thick or too thin. The cannon won't fire if the ball doesn't fit snug inside."

Another man reached for the knife slung into his belt. He slashed a ragged square from the carpet with a harsh tearing sound. Caroline held her breath as the men carefully wrapped one of their cannonballs with the carpet. They held the strange package against the cannon's mouth, checking the size.

"Hurrah!" a gunner cried. Several others cheered.

"It suits?" Caroline asked again.

Mr. Shaw nodded, red-faced and sweaty. "It's perfect!"

Mrs. Shaw grabbed Caroline's hand and pulled

Caroline lifted one edge of the carpet. "Will it suit?" she cried.

her a short distance away.

"May we stay and watch?" Caroline begged.

"Just for a moment," Mrs. Shaw said. She seemed to understand how Caroline felt.

One of the gunners began shouting orders. "Load! Ram home charge! Prime!" Caroline didn't understand all the words, but the gun crew did. Each man had a special job to do as the cannon was readied. *It's almost like watching a dance,* Caroline thought, *where everyone knows the steps.*

"Ready!" the man yelled. A man holding a burning stick stepped forward to light the gunpowder. *"Fire!"*

The cannon boomed. Caroline jumped and clapped her hands over her ears. A sharp smell stung her nose. A cloud of gray smoke appeared.

"Drive them off, boys!" Mrs. Shaw shouted.

"Yes!" Caroline cried. "Drive them off!" Mrs. Shaw grinned at her. Caroline grinned back.

The gun crew didn't waste time cheering. The men were already getting new orders. Step by step, they prepared the cannon to fire again.

Mrs. Shaw took Caroline's hand once more. "We must get back home," she said. "Your grandmother will be worried."

Caroline realized that in her excitement, she had almost forgotten the danger they were in. "Yes," she agreed. "We should go."

Mrs. Shaw held Caroline's hand all the way home. Caroline didn't mind a bit.

"I am so proud of you." Mama put both hands on Caroline's shoulders. "What a clever girl you are! Taking the carpet to the gun crew must have been terribly frightening."

It was late afternoon. The fighting was over. Mama had invited all the shipyard workers home for a picnic supper, and now they sprawled on the lawn. Hosea and Samuel had built a fire and were preparing to roast some trout. Grandmother brought out cornbread and a raspberry cobbler.

Mama's praise made Caroline feel warm inside. "I wasn't frightened until later," she confessed, glancing at Grandmother. "I just wanted to help win the battle."

"And, by heaven, those cannonballs ran the British off!" Mr. Tate said.

Lieutenant Woolsey's men had exchanged fire with the British ships for about two hours. At the shipyard, the men had prepared for a fight, arming themselves with clubs and hammers. Mama had stood with Papa's pistol in her hand, ready to defend the yard. But the British had suddenly lifted anchor and sailed back toward Kingston without landing at all. The American ships in Sackets Harbor were safe.

Mama shook her head. "I was determined that the British would not deny you a carpet to warm your feet this winter," she said. "They did indeed cost you your carpet, but it was a sacrifice well worth making."

Mrs. Shaw, who had come to the celebration with her husband, smiled at Caroline. "We did well, didn't we?"

"We did," Caroline agreed. "We did indeed."

As one of the workers began to tell—for the third time—how he'd climbed to the roof of a shed, ready to drop down on the first British soldier to set foot into the shipyard, Caroline excused herself and walked to her favorite spot overlooking the lake.

So much had happened since the day Papa and Oliver had been taken prisoner! That day she'd stood on this very spot, feeling lost and helpless. Caroline missed Papa and Oliver as much as ever, but she felt a little more hopeful today. She felt proud, too. She'd been able to help the American cause.

Lake Ontario rippled in shades of blue and green below. Caroline could see *Oneida* patrolling nearby. There were no British ships in sight.

"We beat you," Caroline whispered. She knew the war was just beginning. The British would likely come again. But right now, she simply wanted to enjoy her small triumph. "We *beat* you," she said again, staring in the direction of Kingston. "And Papa, wherever you are . . . I'm trying to stay steady and ride out the storm. I'll never stop watching and waiting. And somehow, I'll help find a way to bring you back home."

It was a promise.

LOOKING BACK

AMERICA
IN
1812

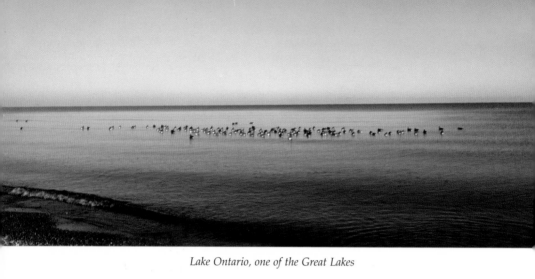

Lake Ontario, one of the Great Lakes

Caroline Abbott lives in Sackets Harbor at the edge of Lake Ontario, a lake so big that when people first see it, they sometimes say it looks like the ocean. If Caroline stood at the water's edge and looked west past the harbor, she would not be able to see the opposite shore.

In the early 1800s, the land around the Great Lakes was America's northern *frontier,* or edge. The land was covered in forests. Small towns like Sackets Harbor were remote and isolated, a great distance away from cities like Philadelphia and New York.

People visiting Sackets Harbor in Caroline's time would have seen boats of all sizes coming and going almost every day. The tall sailing ships were an impressive sight, with white sails billowing in the breeze. Some had pretty carvings

Tall ships like this one traded on the Great Lakes.

called *figureheads* on the *bow*, or front of the boat. Because they were made by hand, no two ships were exactly the same.

Shipbuilders like Caroline's father had good reason to be proud of the sturdy, beautiful ships they built. In Caroline's time, most roads in America were barely better than narrow, muddy paths. It was difficult, expensive, and slow to carry goods by horse-drawn wagon. (Trains did not yet exist.) Boats moved more quickly and could carry large amounts of cargo over rivers and lakes. For this reason, most early settlements, towns, and cities were built near water.

If people needed something that couldn't be made or grown nearby, chances are it would come to them by boat. Ships sailing out of Sackets Harbor carried wheat, pork, and other foods to sell or trade in other parts of America and Upper Canada. Ships sailing into port carried marvelous things from New York, Boston, Baltimore, and even Europe. They brought useful items such as dishes, kettles, hairbrushes, rugs, and fabrics for making clothing. Sometimes they brought luxuries —an ornate mirror, a fancy doll, or maybe even a piano.

When Caroline was a girl, America was young, too. The United States was barely 30 years old and had just

In 1803, the Louisiana Purchase (shown in green) doubled the size of the country.

18 states. But the country was growing. Its population had almost doubled since the end of the Revolutionary War. The nation was much bigger, too. Its land now swept from the Atlantic Ocean to the Rocky Mountains.

Although many Americans were pleased about their country's rapid growth, Britain was not. America had won its independence in the Revolutionary War, but the two countries were not on good terms. Some Americans wanted to expand to the north and take control of Canada, but Britain wanted to protect its claim to the Canadian colonies. Britain also befriended Native Americans, who were angry that U.S. settlers had been taking their land. Many Americans believed that Britain was stirring up trouble on the frontier and encouraging Indians to fight the settlers.

Since the Revolutionary War, the British also had been capturing American sailors at sea and forcing them to serve in the British Navy. Over the years, more than 10,000 men had been kidnapped, leaving their

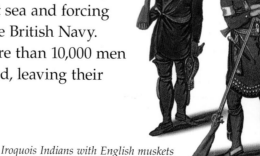

Iroquois Indians with English muskets

*British sailors capturing
American seamen*

children fatherless and
their wives in poverty.
More recently, the
British had begun to
block American ships
from landing in other
countries to trade,
making it much harder
for American farmers, merchants, and tradesmen to sell
their products and earn a living.

Some Americans were very angry at Britain. They
wanted to put Britain in its place. Though many other
Americans disagreed with this plan, the United States
declared war against Britain on June 18, 1812.

News of the war traveled slowly. Many sailors were

*This painting expressed the
feelings of many Americans, who
wanted to remind the British of
their independence.*

caught off guard, just like
Caroline's father and cousin
Oliver. Two brothers, Elijah
and Cyrus St. John, were sailing across Lake Erie, carrying
goods from New York to
Michigan. Before they reached
Michigan, their ship was captured by a Canadian ship,
Queen Charlotte. The men and
their entire crew were prisoners of war before they even
knew a war had begun.

81

The United States was not prepared to fight against Britain, which had the world's most powerful navy. Only one U.S. warship patrolled the vast waters of Lake Ontario. But the Americans knew that for the British to get provisions and military supplies to their forts on the Great Lakes, they had to cross Lake Ontario. That meant whoever controlled Lake Ontario would control a key supply route—and could win the war. The United States would need more ships, and fast.

Word went out. More than a thousand shipbuilders, sailmakers, carpenters, and sailors hurried to Sackets Harbor to help build and sail a fleet. A small shipyard like Abbott's would suddenly have become extremely busy!

The war made life very different for the people who called Sackets Harbor home. The streets were filled with strangers.

The real Lieutenant Woolsey of the U.S. Navy, who appears in the story

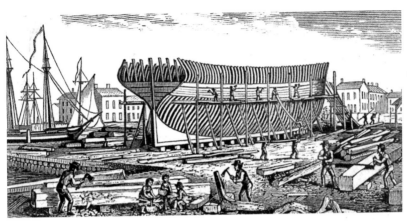

A ship under construction

The air was filled with the sounds of sawing and hammering and sometimes the echoing booms of cannon fire. A girl gazing out from the water's edge would no longer see only peaceful ships bringing goods from far-away cities. Now she would see something much more frightening: fierce warships fitted with rows of cannons ready to do battle.

A SNEAK PEEK AT

Caroline's
SECRET MESSAGE

*Caroline and Mama make a dangerous journey
to the British fort where Papa is held prisoner.
Will they be able to help him escape?*

Mama began to row the skiff through the harbor. Several honking geese flew past. Caroline heard sailors on a nearby schooner bellowing "Heave, heave, heave!" as they raised a sail. Perhaps they would head out to search for British ships. *And we're heading out on a dangerous trip, too,* Caroline thought.

Once they reached the open lake Mama paused, shrugging her shoulders to ease her muscles. "The wind is perfect today," she said.

Caroline lifted her face and tried to consider the wind against her cheeks as Papa had taught her. "The breeze seems strong, but not *too* strong," she agreed. "Shall we set the sail?"

As Caroline raised the sail, her spirits lifted, too. She hadn't traveled on Lake Ontario in all the months since the British had captured Papa. In spite of her worries, being back on the water made her happy. She closed her eyes for a moment, feeling the skiff bob on the choppy water. *Papa will come home,* Caroline told herself. She'd prove herself steady enough to make a good captain. And one day Papa would build a sloop just for her.

As Caroline raised the sail, her spirits lifted, too. She hadn't traveled on
Lake Ontario in all the months since the British had captured Papa.

The skiff rose on a little wave and then dropped again. Caroline's eyes flew open as an icy spray of water hit her face.

"Try not to get splashed," Mama warned. Her cheeks were already bright red from cold.

Caroline wiped her cheek with one hand. The wind that filled their sail also knifed through her cloak. This was a dangerous time of year to travel in such a small boat. If a storm blew up and swamped the little skiff, she and Mama might freeze before reaching shore or getting rescued.

"I'll stay dry," Caroline promised. "Knowing that Papa built this skiff makes me feel safe. It's almost as if he's here, taking care of us. And maybe Papa will soon be sailing it himself!"

Mama smiled. "That's a lovely thought."

As they settled in for the long journey, Caroline found her mind bouncing between thoughts of Papa and thoughts of the quarrel she'd had with Rhonda that morning. *You can mend things with Rhonda when you get home,* Caroline told herself. Still, Rhonda's comments echoed in her mind.

"Mama," Caroline said finally, "Mr. Tate said you'd invited him to my birthday dinner."

"I did," Mama said. "I want the evening to be special."

Caroline heard Rhonda's voice again: *How nice that you have someone to take your father's place.* "All I want is Papa home for my birthday," Caroline said.

Mama's face softened. "We both want that, and I pray that he will be. But even if he isn't, we'll have a real party. Now that the Hathaways have come, there will be lots of people to celebrate your birthday."

Caroline looked out over the restless water. "I think . . . that is, I'd rather have just family at my birthday dinner."

"I see," Mama said slowly. "I thought it would be nice for you to have another girl in the house. Don't you like Rhonda?"

"I don't want another girl in the house," Caroline grumbled. She felt tears threaten and blinked hard to hold them back. "And Mr. Tate can never take Papa's place!"

Mama looked startled. "Of *course* not! But today, let's think just about getting Papa home, shall we?"

Caroline's cheeks grew hot with embarrassment. She was determined to be helpful on this trip.

Fretting about her quarrel with Rhonda wouldn't help anything.

"Yes," she agreed firmly. "Let's think just about getting Papa home."

The trip took all day. Mama sailed close to shore as they traveled, threading their way around islands. She landed the skiff several times on deserted beaches so that she and Caroline could stretch their legs, rub their arms for warmth, and snack on bread and apples.

Caroline felt that knotted feeling in her stomach again as they reached the north shore of the Saint Lawrence River. That mighty river marked the border between New York and Upper Canada. *We're in enemy territory now,* she thought. She couldn't see any British ships, but she knew they must be patrolling nearby.

As Caroline watched the wooded shoreline of Upper Canada glide by, she imagined Papa slipping away from his guards and hiding in the forest. Sometimes she and Mama sailed past Indian camps or little clearings where settlers had built log homes. The shelters and cabins looked no different from those Caroline knew in New York. It seemed so strange to think that the people who lived in them were likely loyal to the British!

Finally Mama said, "We're getting close to Uncle Aaron and Aunt Martha's farm. You've done well today, Caroline."

Mama's praise made Caroline feel good, and she was glad she hadn't complained about the cold or her growing hunger. Still, by the time the cabin came into view a few miles east of Kingston, Caroline felt hollow and frozen to the bone. Her arms ached from helping with the oars. She used her last bit of strength to help Mama pull the skiff up on the shore.